KT-494-944

Disney

First edition

Published by Ladybird Books Ltd  Loughborough  Leicestershire  UK

Printed in England (3)

# WINNIE THE POOH
## and too much honey

Ladybird Books

## Christopher Robin and Pooh

Winnie the Pooh and Christopher Robin were great friends. They lived in a wonderful world of their own, where grown-ups never came. It was called the Hundred Acre Wood, in the middle of the Forest, and lots of other friends lived there too.

There was Piglet, Kanga, Roo, Eeyore, Tigger and Rabbit, and they all knew one another very well.

Sometimes Winnie the Pooh was called Pooh Bear, and other times just Bear or Pooh. He often had adventures in the Hundred Acre Wood, but what Pooh liked most of all was eating honey – as much as he could get.

Pooh always liked honey for his elevenses. He called it, Time for a Little Something.

One day, the honey pot was empty. Christopher Robin had forgotten to fill it. Pooh was quite cross.

Trying to forget how hungry he was, Pooh made his way to an old tree trunk. It was one of his Thoughtful Spots where he always did his best to think really hard. But it wasn't easy, especially when he was hungry.

Today, though, the thoughts came buzzing. Then... "That's not my thoughts at all," said Pooh. "It's a bee."

And that made him think about honey again, because bees make honey.

## A Little Something
## with Rabbit

Pooh stood up and looked around. He was still thinking. *Someone* in the Forest must have some honey. Then all of a sudden he thought of Rabbit.

Rabbit always had honey, and he usually had a Little Something himself for elevenses.

"I'll go and see Rabbit," Pooh said aloud. "He's sure to have some honey."

He began to walk towards Rabbit's house – and Rabbit heard him coming. "Help!" he thought. "If Pooh knows I'm in, he'll eat all my honey."

So he kept very quiet when Pooh called, "Anyone at home?"

Pooh waited a moment, but when there was no answer, he called once more, "Rabbit, are you there?"

Again Rabbit didn't answer. But when Pooh called a third time, Rabbit said, ''No, there's no one here.''

Pooh was puzzled. How could anyone say, ''No, there's no one here,'' if there *was* no one there?

So he looked inside the hole, and the first thing he saw was Rabbit.

''Hallo, Rabbit,'' he said. ''Just thought I'd pop round to see you.''

Rabbit was always polite. "Hello, Pooh," he said. "How nice to see you. I was just going to have my elevenses. Would you like a Little Something?"

"Oh, how kind of you, Rabbit," said Pooh. "Come to think of it, it *is* about time."

"What would you like?" asked Rabbit. "Some bread and honey, or would you prefer condensed milk?"

"Just honey will do nicely," said Pooh, settling down at the table. "I'm very fond of honey."

Rabbit went over to the cupboard and took out his pot of honey. It was nearly full, because Rabbit had been saving it as a treat.

He carried it across to the table and gave some to Pooh. Pooh looked down at his plate, disappointed. "Could I have a little more, do you think?'' he asked.

Rabbit thumped the pot down on the table. ''You'd better help yourself, I suppose,'' he said.

''Why, thank you, Rabbit,'' said Pooh.

It was one of the best
elevenses Pooh had ever
had. His Little Something
turned into a very Big
Something in the end.

At last Pooh said,
"Well, it's about time I
was going, Rabbit."

"Don't you want any
more, Pooh?" asked
Rabbit.

"I don't think there's
any left," said Pooh.

Rabbit turned the pot
upside down. "No,
you're right," he said
sadly.

"I didn't think there
was," said Pooh.
"Goodbye, and thank
you very much." And he
began to climb out of
Rabbit's hole.

## Half In, Half Out

The next moment, all Rabbit could see was Pooh's fat little legs waving in the air. He was stuck fast in the doorway!

Pooh shouted back to Rabbit, "Why don't you have a bigger front door? Now look what's happened!"

Rabbit was really cross. "It's just the right size for me. Anyway, you got in all right. It's your own fault, Pooh, for being so greedy. If you hadn't eaten all that honey, you wouldn't be stuck now."

Pooh went on trying as hard as he could to get out, but it was no use. After a minute or two he asked hopefully, "Rabbit, do you think you could give me a push?"

Rabbit sighed. He was so cross with Pooh for eating all his honey that he didn't want to help at all. But he pushed and pushed as hard as he could for ages. It was no good.

Then he went out of his back door and round to the front of the house to try to pull Pooh out. That was no good either.

Nothing was going to get Pooh
through that front door. At last Rabbit
gave up.

"There's only one thing for it," he
said. "I'd better see if Christopher
Robin can help." And he ran off to find
him.

Left to himself, Pooh felt quite lonely. And it was no fun at all being stuck in Rabbit's doorway, underneath the sign saying:

RABBit'2
HOWSE

"What on earth are you doing there, Pooh?" asked Owl, flying down to Rabbit's doorway. "You're not stuck, are you?"

"Not really," said Pooh airily. "I was just having a little nap."

Owl laughed at him. "That's a fine story," he said. "I can see you're stuck fast. I'd better get someone who can dig you out."

## The Gopher Takes a Look

At that moment, a gopher came along, his big front teeth gleaming in the sunshine.

"Did you say you need someone who knows about digging?" he asked. "Let's see if *I* can help."

He climbed all round Pooh, whose nose twitched unhappily. Pooh had never seen a gopher in the Forest before – where had this one come from?

Once the gopher had taken a good look at the doorway, he stood back, deep in thought. Then he said to Owl, "The main problem here is this Bear. It's his fault that no one can get in or out."

Pooh growled deep in his throat. The gopher moved back a step and Pooh said, slowly and carefully, "It doesn't matter *whose* fault it is. Can...you... get...me...out?"

"Oh, I just dig," said the gopher hurriedly. "I don't know anything about getting Bears out."

And with that, he disappeared.

## Help Is at Hand!

Now Pooh began to get worried. He was getting very tired of looking at the same view all the time. Was he going to be stuck here for ever, never again to wander

in the Forest, looking for honey?
Where, oh where, was Christopher
Robin?

Pooh's greatest friend was on his way
and soon he was talking to Pooh.

"It's all right," said Christopher
Robin. "We'll soon have you out."

First, Christopher Robin pulled all by himself. Then Rabbit helped him, but it was still no good. Pooh was stuck fast, and nothing – absolutely nothing – was going to move him.

In the end, when it began to rain, Christopher Robin gave up. "I don't know what we're going to do, Pooh," he said. "We're certainly not going to get you out by pulling."

He looked down at Pooh as he thought about the problem. ''There's only one way to do it – and you're not going to like it, Pooh. You will just have to stay there until you get thin again.''

Rabbit was nearly as unhappy as Pooh when he went back into his house and saw Pooh's legs still waving in the air.

"If he's going to be there for months," he thought, "I'm going to have to do something about it. It's hardly a beautiful sight."

Suddenly he had an idea. "I know," he said to himself, "I'll make him into a picture."

So he put a frame round Pooh's back end, and put a flower on his bottom. Then he changed his mind and painted a face on Pooh's bottom, and added twigs to make antlers.

Rabbit was feeling pleased with himself when the picture was finished. He thought it was quite good!

## Kanga and Roo Come Visiting

While Rabbit was painting his picture, Kanga and Roo

had heard Pooh was in trouble, and they'd come to visit him. Roo had

brought him some flowers.

When Pooh saw that they hadn't brought him anything to eat he wasn't as grateful for the flowers as he should have been. Waiting to grow thinner was boring, and it was making him distinctly cross.

All the same, he knew his friends were being very kind, so he did his best to be polite and admire their present.

### Someone to Talk to

Kanga and Roo stayed with Pooh until teatime, then they set off home. The thought of tea made Pooh realise how hungry he was. Then he had to stop thinking about that, because it was going to be a long, long time before he could have anything to eat again.

Suddenly Pooh heard a rustling noise nearby. What could it be?

It turned out to be Eeyore. "I'll stay with you for a while if you like, Pooh," he offered.

"Oh, thank you, Eeyore," said Pooh gratefully. "That's very kind of you!"

"Well," said Eeyore, "I might as well. My part of the Forest is damp. It's not much better here but at least we can chat."

Pooh was glad Eeyore was there, although Eeyore had never been the most cheerful company in the world.

So Pooh decided it was time for a song, and this is what he sang:

*"Cottleston, Cottleston, Cottleston Pie,*
*A fly can't bird, but a bird can fly.*
*Ask me a riddle and I reply:*
'Cottleston, Cottleston, Cottleston Pie.'

*Cottleston, Cottleston, Cottleston Pie,*
*A fish can't whistle and neither can I.*
*Ask me a riddle and I reply:*
'Cottleston, Cottleston, Cottleston Pie.'

*Cottleston, Cottleston, Cottleston Pie,*
*Why does a chicken, I don't know why.*
*Ask me a riddle and I reply:*
'Cottleston, Cottleston, Cottleston Pie.'"

Pooh enjoyed singing and his song made him feel a lot less gloomy. Eeyore seemed to feel better too. He almost managed to smile.

"That wasn't at all bad, I must say, Pooh," he said. "You're quite good at that sort of thing."

Pooh was encouraged by this, so he made up a little poem about an empty honey pot he had at home.

*"It's very, very funny,*
*'Cos I know I had some honey;*
*'Cos it had a label on,*
    *Saying HUNNY.*

*A goloptious full-up pot too,*
*And I don't know where it's got to,*
*No, I don't know where it's gone –*
    *Well, it's funny."*

By the time Pooh had finished his poem, it was starting to grow cold and dark. Christopher Robin came along with a scarf to keep Pooh's ears warm.

"I'm awfully bored, Christopher Robin," said Pooh gloomily. "There must be *something* I can do while I'm stuck here. Can *you* think of anything?"

But it was no good. Christopher Robin couldn't think of a single thing to help.

Even with Eeyore to keep him company, the cold dark night seemed never-ending. But at last the sun rose, and Christopher Robin and all Pooh's friends gathered round to see if they could help.

At Pooh's other end, Rabbit was inside his house, having breakfast. Suddenly he saw Pooh move, and he rushed through his back door and round to tell the others.

"Perhaps I'll get my front door back now," he thought.

Everyone gathered round to take a good look at Pooh, and tried to remember what he had looked like before. *Was* he thinner?

Then they decided – yes, he *was*!

## Pooh Is Set Free

"Now, what's the best way to get Pooh out?" wondered

Christopher Robin. "I know, I'll put my foot on the bank like this, and you stand behind me, Rabbit. Then we'll both pull together."

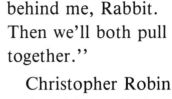

Christopher Robin and Rabbit pulled as hard as they could, but Pooh stayed stuck.

Then everyone else got behind Rabbit in a long line, and pulled as well. That did the trick.

POP! Pooh flew straight into the air and into the honey tree – head first!

Pooh looked round happily. "I don't mind a bit being stuck here for a while with all this lovely honey," he thought. "It's not at all like being stuck in Rabbit's doorway."

Then he suddenly remembered that he hadn't had anything to eat for a very long time. The honey tree was just the place for him!

## Pooh Stays Put

Down below, Pooh's friends were wondering how to get him out once more.

Then Christopher Robin climbed up to talk to him.

"I'm quite happy here for the moment, Christopher Robin," Pooh said stickily. "This is the nicest honey I've ever tasted."

"All right, Pooh, we'll let you stay here just now – but only for a *little* while. And you must only have a *Little* Something, you know."

"Oh, I will," promised Pooh. He didn't want to be stuck in the tree for ever – but it *was* nice honey!

Pooh was quite greedy really. He ate all the honey he could – and that was much more than a Little Something.

When Christopher Robin got him down from the tree at last, Pooh was so full he could hardly walk. But he was so happy that he sang his favourite song:

*"Winnie the Pooh, Winnie the Pooh!*
*Tubby little cubby all stuffed*
  *with fluff!*
*I'm Winnie the Pooh, Winnie the*
  *Pooh!*
*Willy-nilly silly old Bear!"*

For the rest of his life, Winnie the Pooh was going to remember the time he had eaten so much honey that he ended up in a very tight spot indeed.

There are many more stories about Pooh, and other friends to meet.

Grown-ups think that all these stories are make-believe, and that Christopher Robin's friends are only stuffed toys. But you and I know better, don't we?

Of course we do – as sure as there's a Hundred Acre Wood!